Dear God, Can I get a raincheck?

By: Tonya Renee

The sound of running through a once quiet house is met by a voice in the distance.

"Slow down Henry Lee!"

"Sorry mom, got to get to the treehouse. I don't want to be late," he replies.

His mother assures him he has plenty of time before he trots out the backdoor kicking up dust.

She makes her way to the door and watches as her son climbs up into his treehouse. Their dog stands at the door whimpering.

"You want to go outside as well Banjo? Ok, keep an eye on Henry for me."

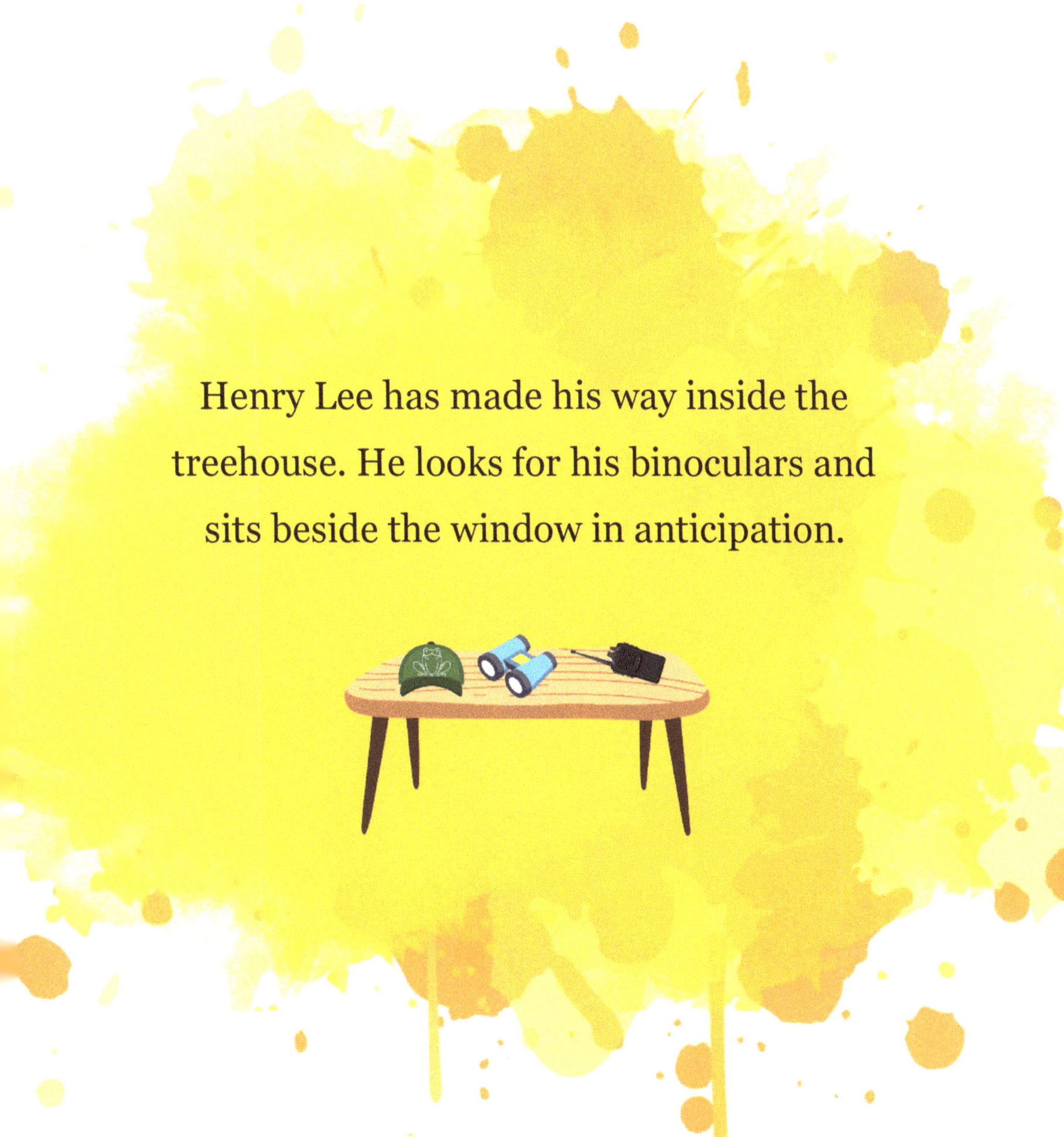

Henry Lee has made his way inside the treehouse. He looks for his binoculars and sits beside the window in anticipation.

Ring, ring, ring from inside the house.
"Hello dear, yes, I will tell him now. Love you
as well, see you when you return."

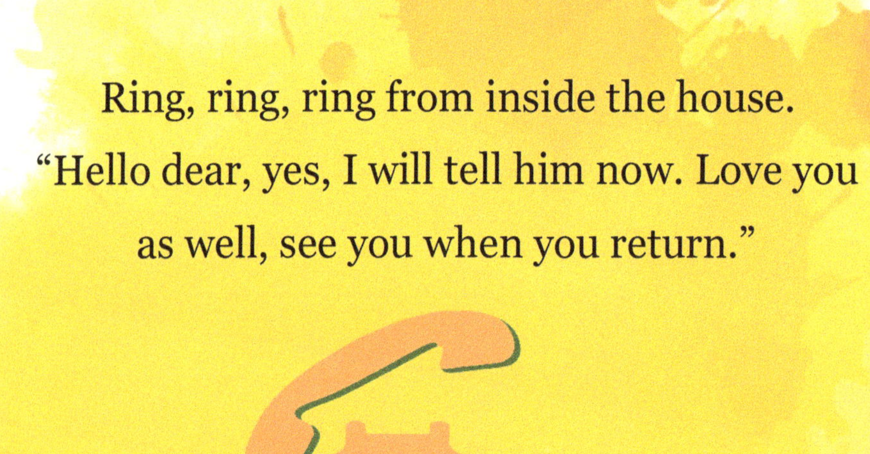

His mother walks over to the counter to a small walkie talkie on standby.

“Mama bear 1,2 Mama bear 1,2 are you there Froggie pond?”

Mama bear this is Froggie pond 1,2.”, Henry replies.

“Papa bear is about to clear the pond 1.2.”, she echoes back over the walkie talkie.

“Froggie pond in position thank you Mom!”, Henry out.

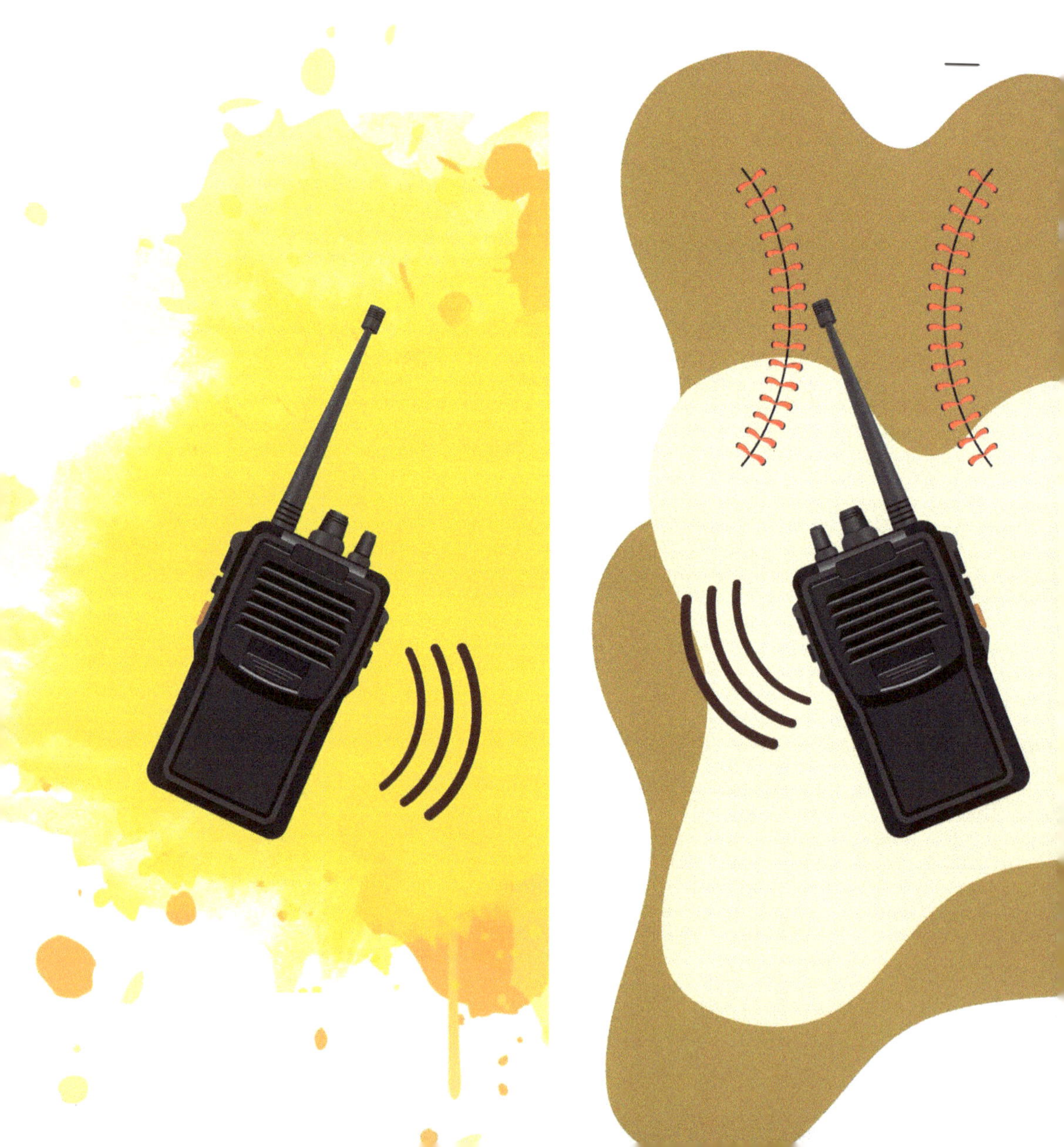

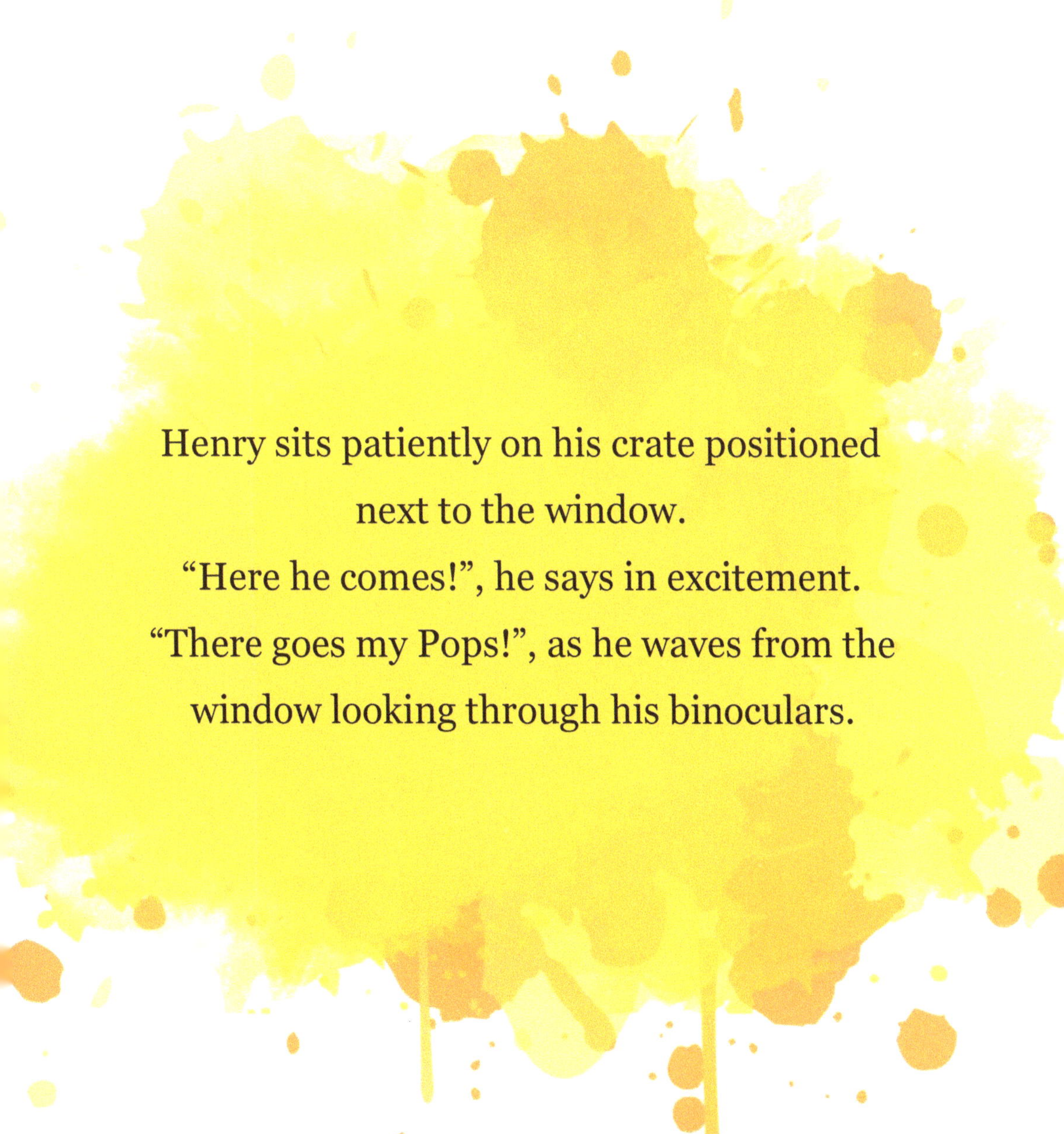

Henry sits patiently on his crate positioned next to the window.

"Here he comes!", he says in excitement.

"There goes my Pops!", as he waves from the window looking through his binoculars.

He looks down below the treehouse and sees
Banjo twirling in excitement as well.
"Yep, Banjo he's flying with the birds.", as he
climbs back to the ground.
Banjo jumps on him excitedly!
"It's ok boy, he'll be back in a few days, and
he will be taking me to my favorite baseball
team's championship game. I can't wait!"

Henry Lee! Come on let's get going."

"Okay mom! On my way. Let's go boy."

He places Banjo back in the house and heads to his mother's car. He climbs in the backseat and straps himself in securely."

Today is one of Henry's favorite days. He and his mother are on their way to Super Duper Market. Henry loves going on trips with his mom because he will get a special treat if he behaves.

Looking out the window, Henry knows they are getting close to their destination by some of the landmarks.

He says to himself, there's the park! His mom usually stops there on the way home, so Henry can look in the pond at the fish and of course the frogs, they are his favorite. He wants a frog as a pet, but his mom said no way!

There's the bank, mom we are almost there."
As they continue, he sees a giant ice cream
cone in the sky, and he knows the ice cream
shop is straight ahead. It sits next to Super
Duper and that's where he will get his treat to
take to the park. He usually sneaks pieces of
his cone in the pond for the fish.

ATM
ATM
BANK
TAXI

Open

"We are here.", his mother says.

He is excited! Good ole Super Duper they got some of everything!

"Ok Henry let's get going. I got my list right here, we are set."

"Mom did you remember my favorite pasta?", he asked.

"Yes dear, it's at the top of the list."

SUPER DUPER
MARKET
24 HOUR
OPEN
Supermarket
24 hrs
SUPER DUPER
MARKET
P

"Super Duper is huge!", Henry responded.

Henry always makes sure to stay in close proximity to the cart as they walk through the store. He told his mother once if he got lost in Super Duper, he would be ok, because they have plenty to eat in the store. She told him how sad they would be because they would not be able to find him.

Because of that he would always hold on to the shopping cart because he never wanted to make them sad, even though he could survive on the candy isles.

SUPER
DUPER
sales
SALE
SALE
SALE
SALE
SALE
SALE

After making their way through the store, their last stop is the pasta. When they get there Henry's favorite pasta is sold out.

"Oh no!", she says.

"What is it?", he replies.

"They are out of your favorite pasta. You will have to get a few cans of the dinosaurs until they restock."

Sadly, he says," ok".

SUPER DUPER MARKET
SOLD OUT
SUPER SALE
5/ $1
Ravioli Pasta
SALE!

She looks at Henry's face and reassures him it will be ok.

"Don't worry dear we will stock up next time. I will get a raincheck so we can get them the next time we are here."

"Raincheck?", puzzled Henry says.

"Let's go checkout so we can go get your ice cream and head to the park."

"Ok!", he responds.

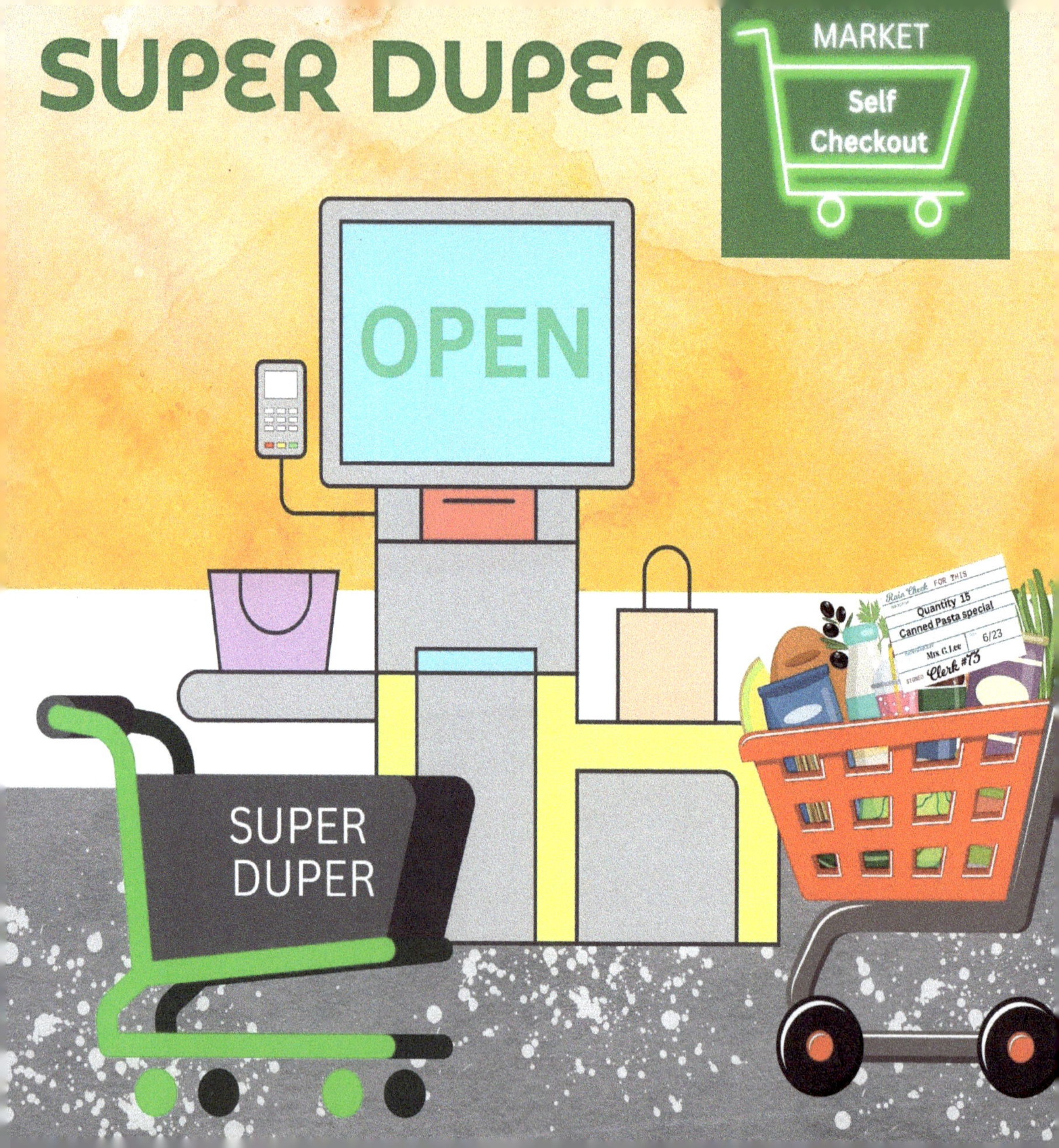
SUPER DUPER
MARKET
Self
Checkout
OPEN
SUPER
DUPER
Rain Check FOR THIS
Quantity 15
Canned Pasta special
Mrs G. Lee
6/23
SIGNED Clerk #73

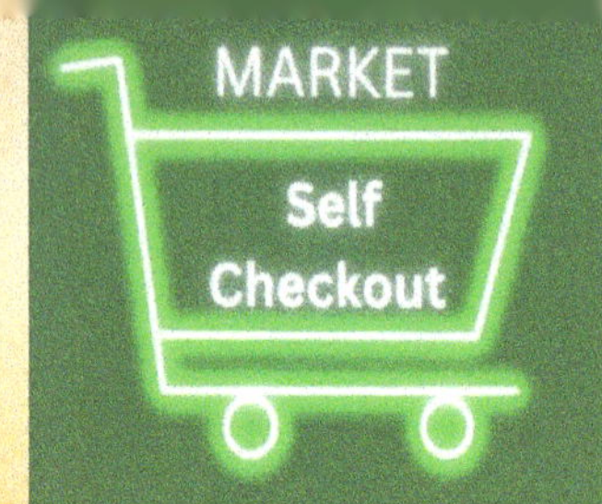

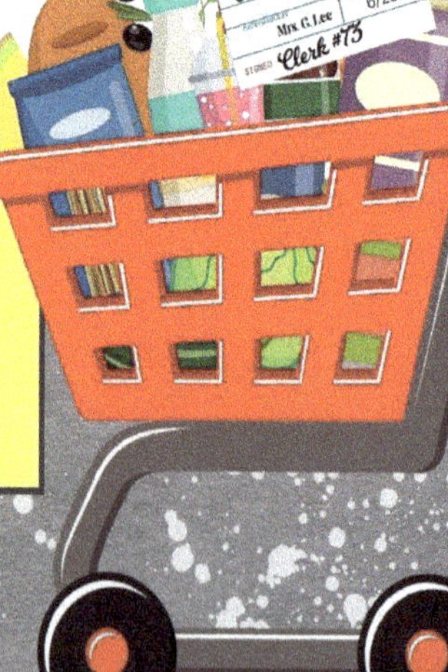

Henry and his mom stopped for his treat and made their way to the park.

At the park Henry asks his mother, "Mom, what is a raincheck?"

She explains, "A raincheck allows me to get something later that I was supposed to get today."

"So, you will get my today pasta another day?"

Smiling she says, "Yes that's the plan."

Henry and his mother make it back home
after a long day. They order pizza and watch
one of their favorite movies before heading to
bed because Henry has school, and she has to
work in the morning.

Early the next day, like clockwork Henry's mom is up and ready for work. She prepares breakfast and tidies up as she waits for Henry to finish getting ready for school. She drops him off at school and his grandmother usually picks him up when dad works out of town.

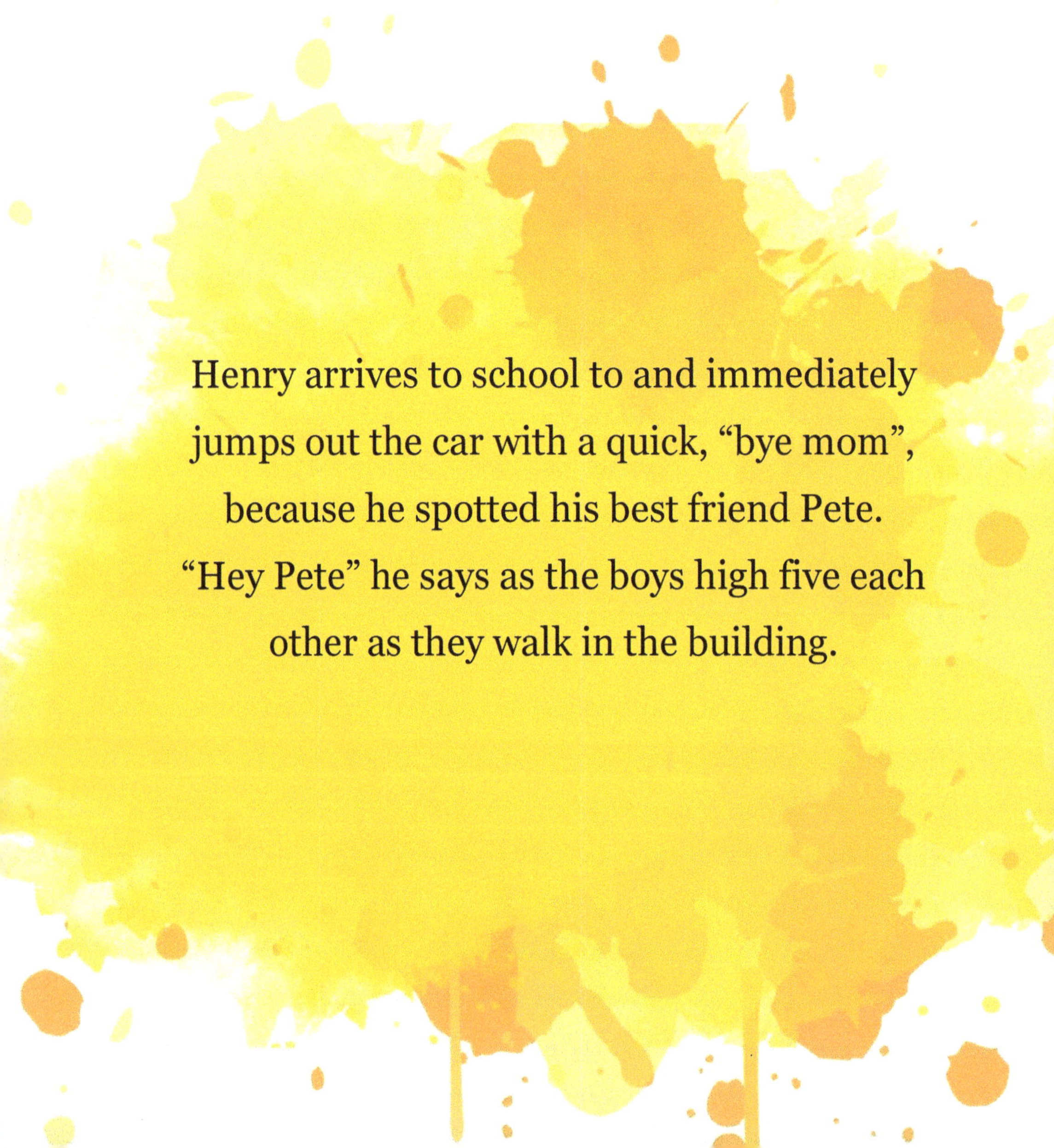

Henry arrives to school to and immediately jumps out the car with a quick, "bye mom", because he spotted his best friend Pete. "Hey Pete" he says as the boys high five each other as they walk in the building.

SCHOOL
244
SCHOOL BUS
0114
0114

At recess Pete took one of Henry's most prized possessions, a frog key ring he carries on his backpack. His dad bought it for him from one of his trips. Pete has the key chain locked in his grip and takes off running. Before you know it the two boys are tussling in the dirt and create a total commotion on the playground.

OH!
OOUPS!
VS
POW!
OUCH!

The teacher immediately pulls the boys apart and Henry has the key chain tucked in his hand. Both of the boys are sent to the nurse's office to get checked before reporting to the principal's office. The boys sit outside the nurse's office and apologize to each other for getting one another in trouble.

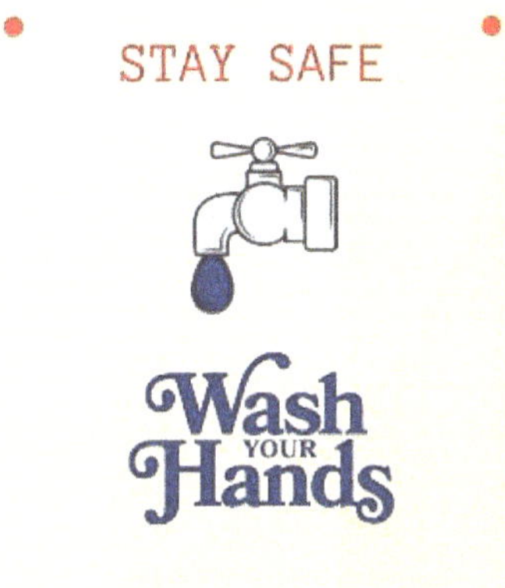

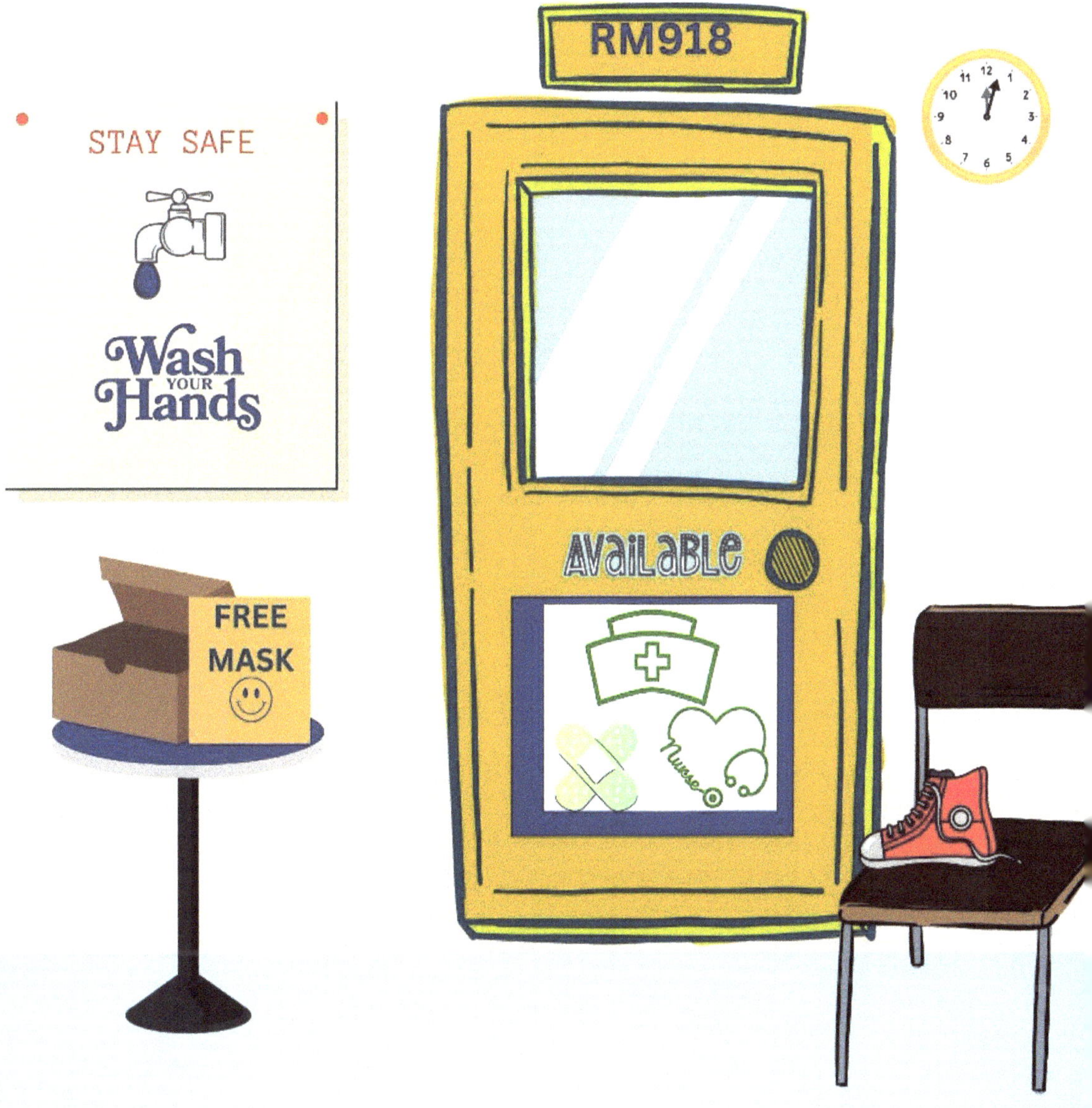
RM918
STAY SAFE
Wash YOUR Hands
AVAILABLE
FREE MASK
Nurse

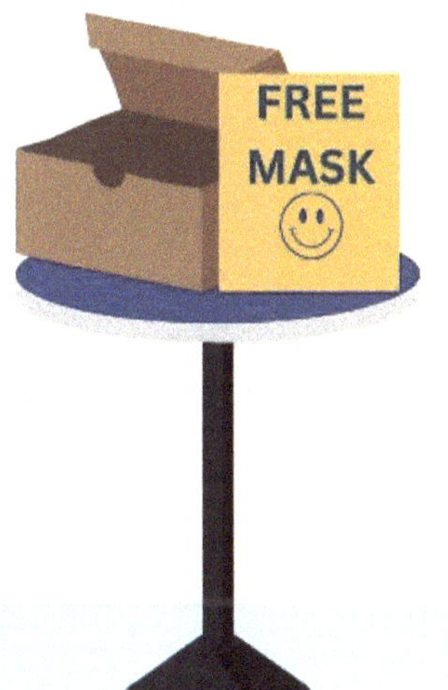

Inside the principal's office, they explained they were just playing, and that they would never fight, they are best friends. The principal explains that he would still have to contact their parents and explain today's incident. Henry and Pete made their way back to class laughing and still best friends.

Knowledge
is
Power

After school Henry's granny picks him up in her pickup truck. She usually grabs him and her a sandwich from the local deli market.

SCHOOL
207
delivery
0302 SCHOOL BUS 0302
0225 SCHOOL BUS 0225

When he gets home, he changes from his school clothes and begins to think about the call that his mother will receive from the school. He gets an idea to make his mother a treat. His mother often would make cookie mug treats in the microwave.

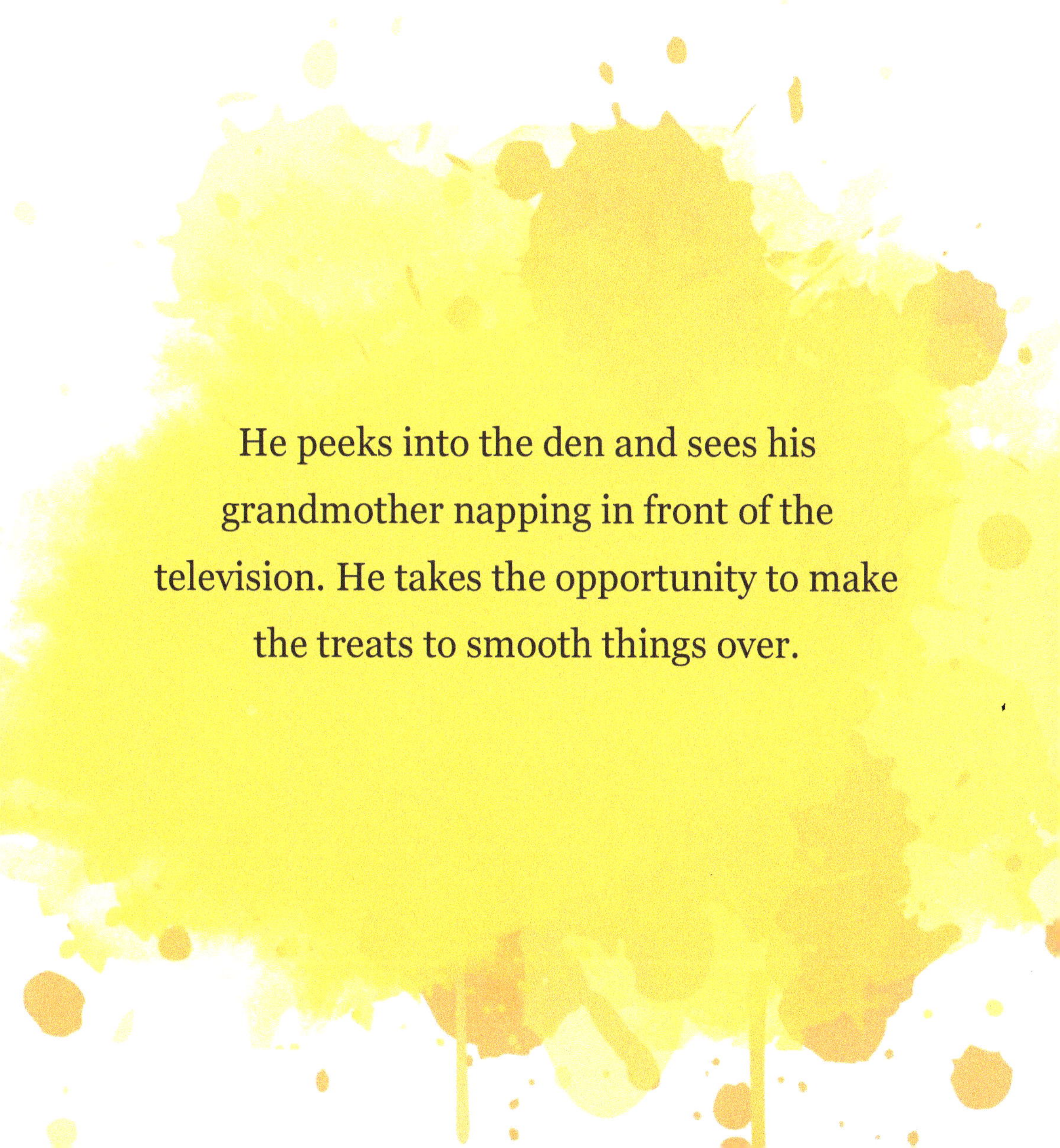

He peeks into the den and sees his grandmother napping in front of the television. He takes the opportunity to make the treats to smooth things over.

8
MOVIE
TIME

He makes a mess!

Banjo sits in amazement as well.

"Henry! What are you doing?", his mother asks.

"Mommy, I was making you a treat.", with a smile on his face and flour on his nose.

"Look at this mess though, Henry!", sternly speaking.

He immediately grabs the broom and tries to clean up the mess he has created.

Sugar
FLOUR
MILK

"Does this have anything to do with the phone call from school today?"

"Maybe", he softly speaks.

"What happened?"

"It was a misunderstanding that's all. You know how Pete is, mom, he's my best friend and I apologized. He took my keychain and ran.", he explains.

"Well, we will ask your father what he thinks.
I think your punishment should be no
baseball championship."
"Mom, please not that.", he pleads.
"We will let your father decide, ok?"
"Ok", he responds in sadness.
He never thought his game was in jeopardy.
After cleaning up his mess in the kitchen, he
went to his room to ponder over the situation.

Later that evening he hears the phone ring in

the next room and his mother calls his name.

"Your dad wants to speak with you."

"Ok", Henry takes the phone, "Hi dad".

"Hi buddy what's this your mom tells me about you and Petey."

Quickly he responds, "Dad it was just us horseplaying and it got out of hand. We are still best buds and we both apologized. Please don't take my ticket!"

"Calm down, calm down!"

"Let's let God decide.", his dad says.

"God?", Henry looks puzzled on the phone.

DAD HOME

"Yes, you pray about it and see what God says. he explains. Whatever the answer he gives you I will accept."

"But daddy how will I know his answer?"

"Believe me son you will know. I will be home in a few days, and you can tell me what he said."

"Ok, dad."

Henry goes and sits on the sofa with his mom still looking puzzled. "What did your dad decide?"

"He didn't.", he replies.

"He didn't?", now she looks puzzled.

He said, "I should let God decide!"

"Oh really!", with a smile of satisfaction on her face.

"Mama, I don't know what to say."

"You pray to God at night, don't you?", she asked.

"Yeah, but this is different."

"Is it?", she responds.

"When you go to bed talk to him like you are talking to me. It's that simple, he wants us to talk to him, not just before we go to sleep or blessing our food but always because he loves us, and he is concerned about us."

"Really?"

"Yes, really!"

She grabs her bible from the table and reads him a scripture, "Ask and it will be given to you, seek (look for), and you will find, knock and it will be opened to you. (Matthew 7:7) You understand?"

Henry looks at his mother and nods, "yes I understand."

They watch television a little longer and
Henry tells his mom he has to go to bed early
because God might have a lot of
appointments tonight and he doesn't want to
be placed on hold too long.
She laughs and says, "Ok dear goodnight."

YOU
ARE
A
CHAMPION!
HENRY LEE

Henry goes to his room and changes into his favorite pj's. He says to himself, "that maybe if God knows how much he likes the Froggies that he will let him still go to the game." Henry's mother out of curiosity steps behind his door so she is not seen but can listen as he talks with God.

Hi! Dad

Henry Lee kneels down next to his bed and begins to {{KNOCK}} on the tabletop next to his bed.

"Hi, God, it's me Henry Lee I knocked first I hope you're here. Mom said, I should just talk to you like I talk to her. She probably knows I have heard her talk to you before. Well, I'm sure you know why I'm here. I got in trouble today with my buddy, you know Pete.

Long story short, I don't want to hold up the line.

Henry's mom snickers in amazement behind the door.

"Dad said you can decide, I really want to go to the game. So, what I am asking, God I know I deserve it, but can I get a raincheck?

Henry's mother stands in amazement of her little man.

Henry continues, "Well I guess that's all. Continue to bless my family and everyone on the plane with my daddy that they make it home safely. Oh yes, can you give Pete a raincheck as well. He is my best friend. Thanks again, this is Henry Lee out 1,2,1,2."

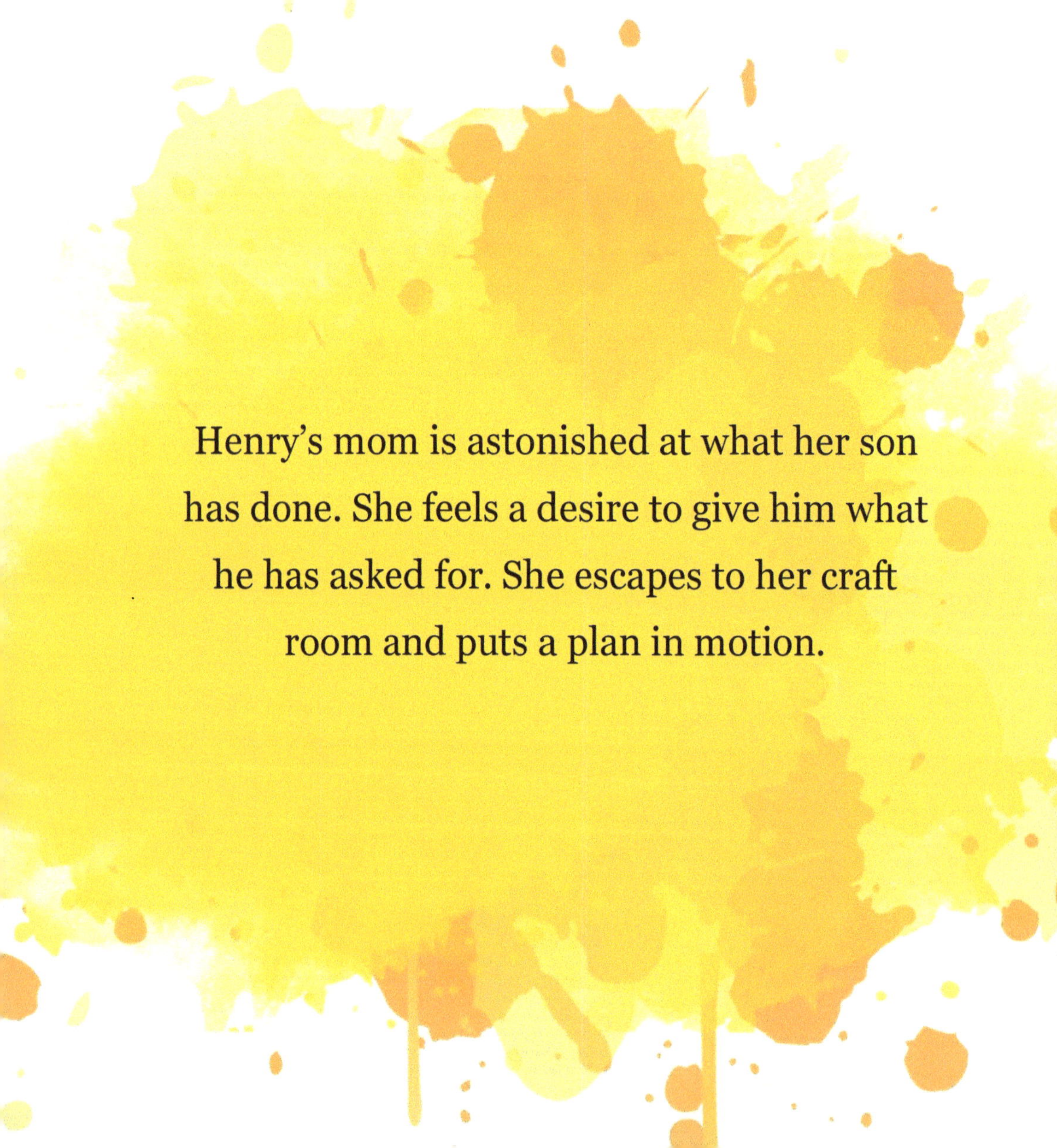

Henry's mom is astonished at what her son
has done. She feels a desire to give him what
he has asked for. She escapes to her craft
room and puts a plan in motion.

Live
Creatively

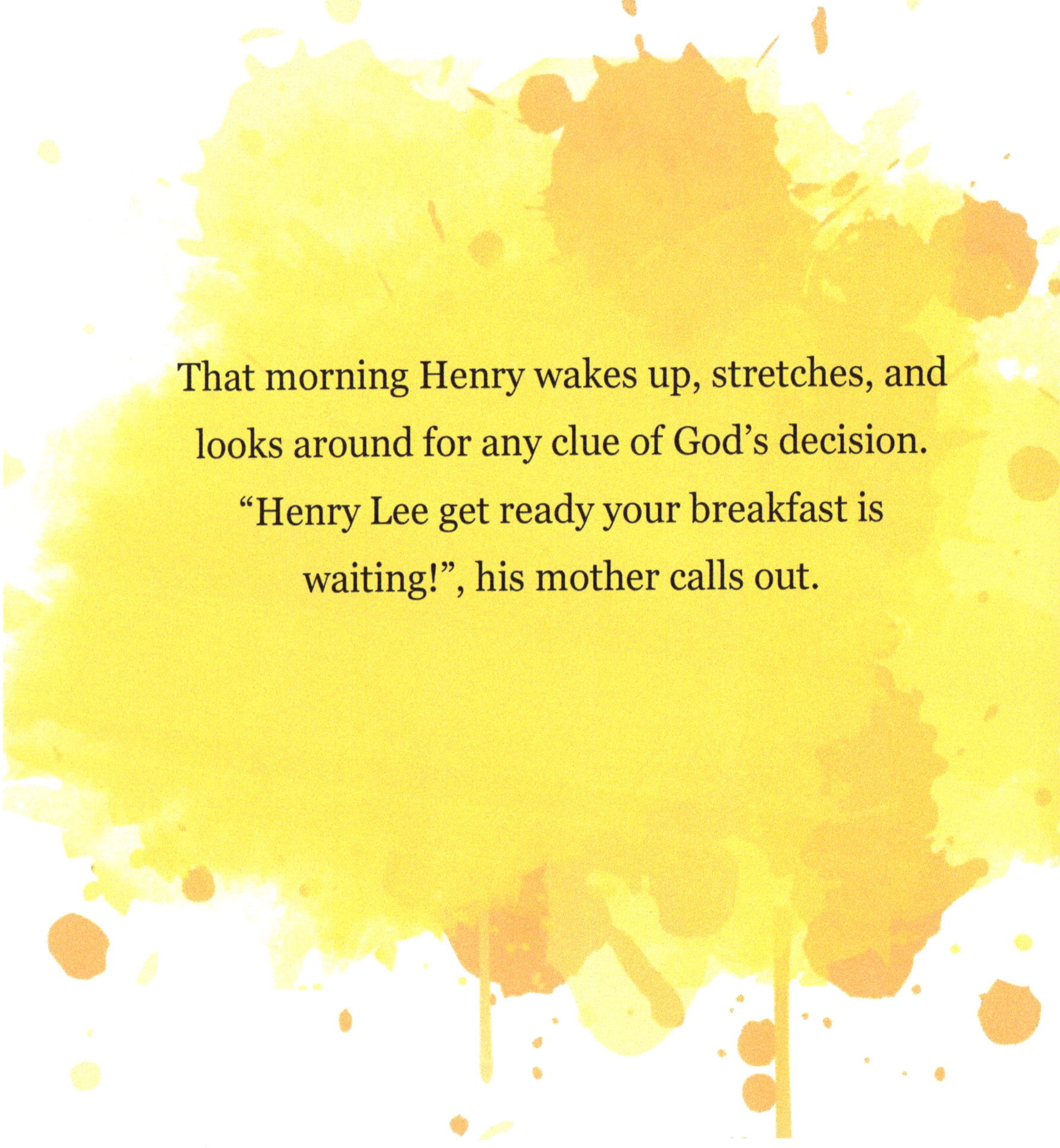
That morning Henry wakes up, stretches, and looks around for any clue of God's decision. "Henry Lee get ready your breakfast is waiting!", his mother calls out.

He does as she says and makes his way to the kitchen. As he approaches, he notices a package sitting on top of the counter and the label says Henry Lee.
He picks it up and shakes it but no sound. It is light as a feather.

cereal
MILK
For
Henry Lee

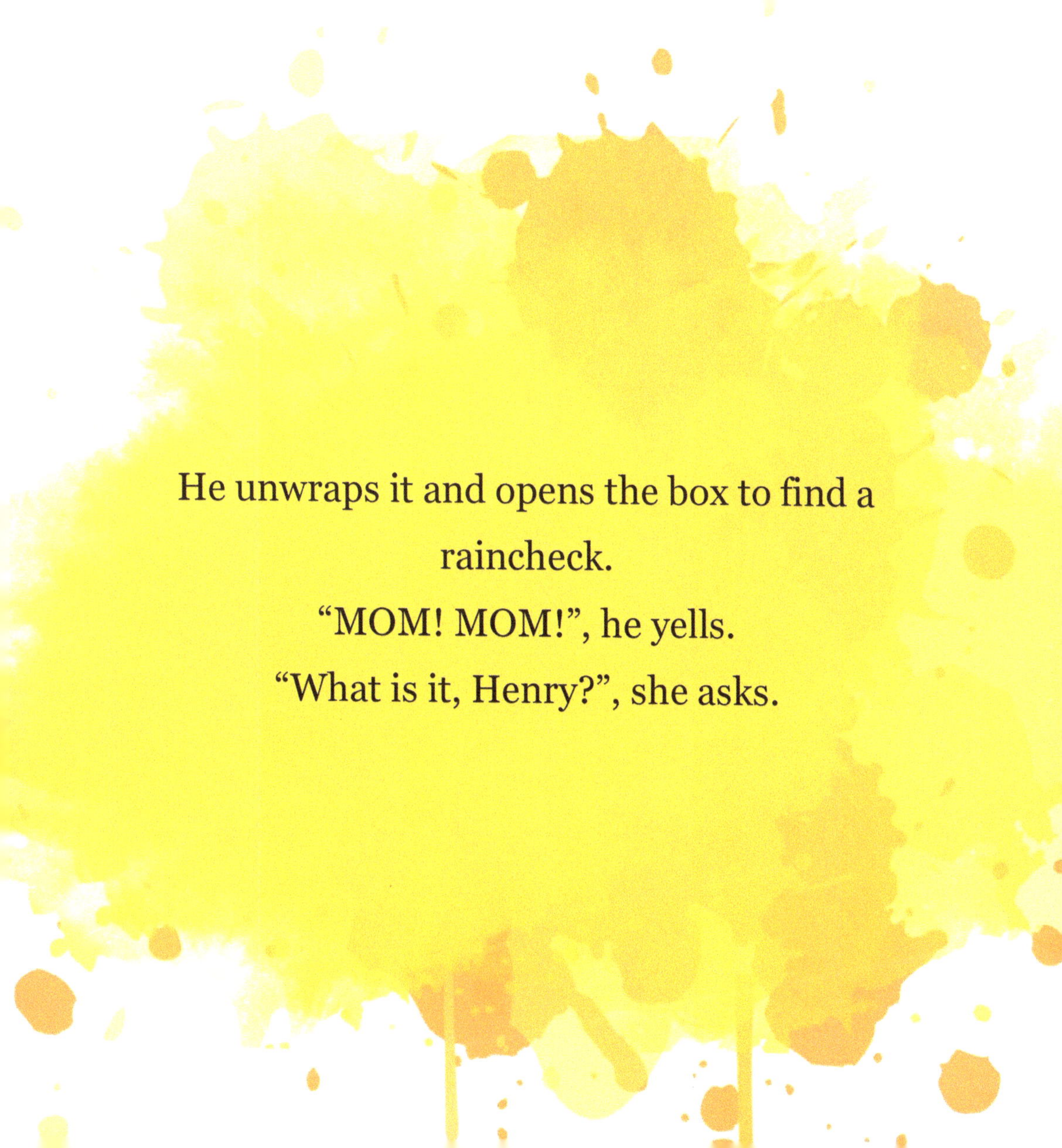

He unwraps it and opens the box to find a
raincheck.

"MOM! MOM!", he yells.

"What is it, Henry?", she asks.

For
Henry Lee

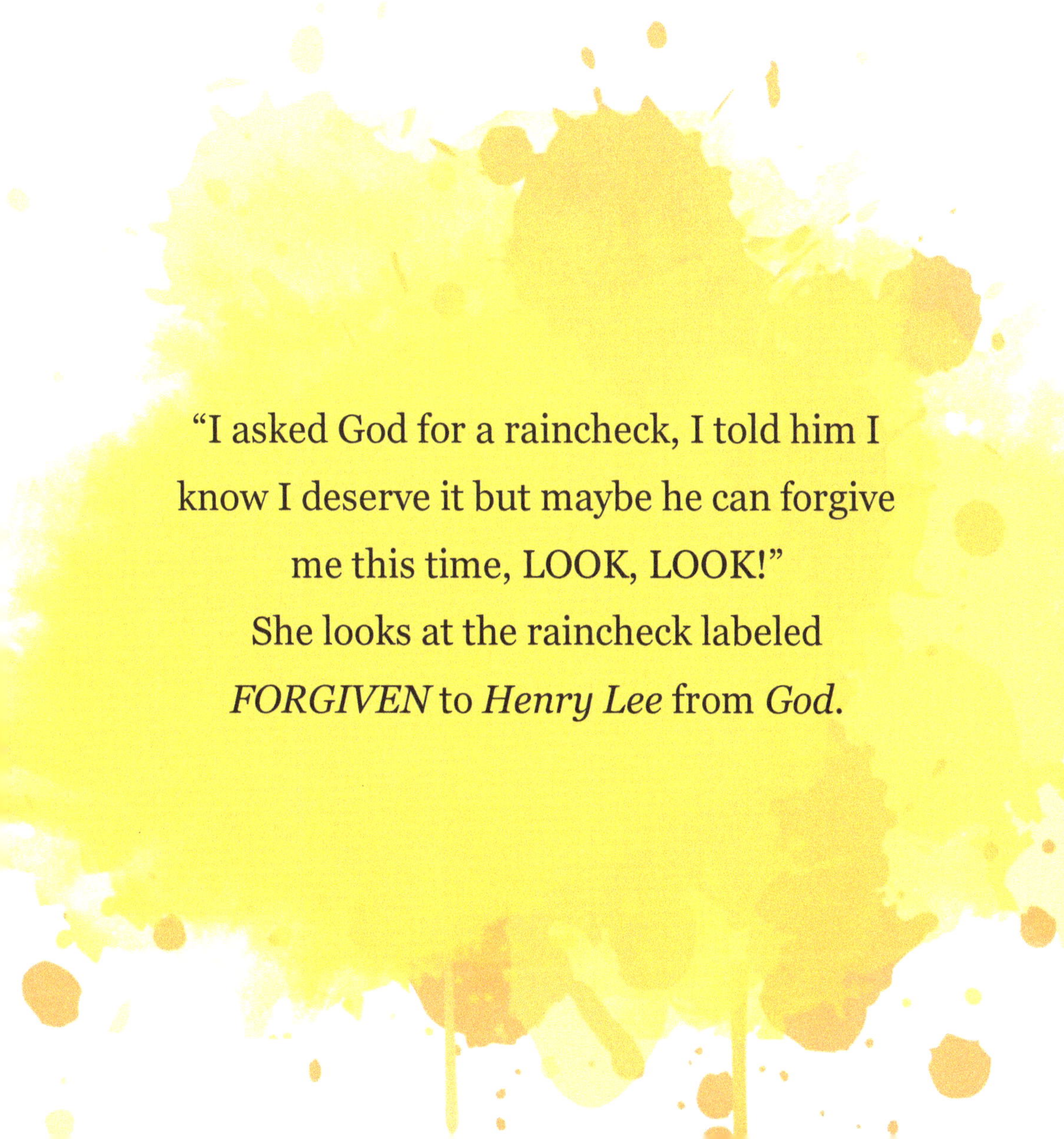

"I asked God for a raincheck, I told him I know I deserve it but maybe he can forgive me this time, LOOK, LOOK!"
She looks at the raincheck labeled FORGIVEN to Henry Lee from God.

Rain Check FOR THIS
GOOD FOR
FORGIVEN
REDEEMABLE BY
Henry Lee
Date
SIGNED God
For Henry Lee

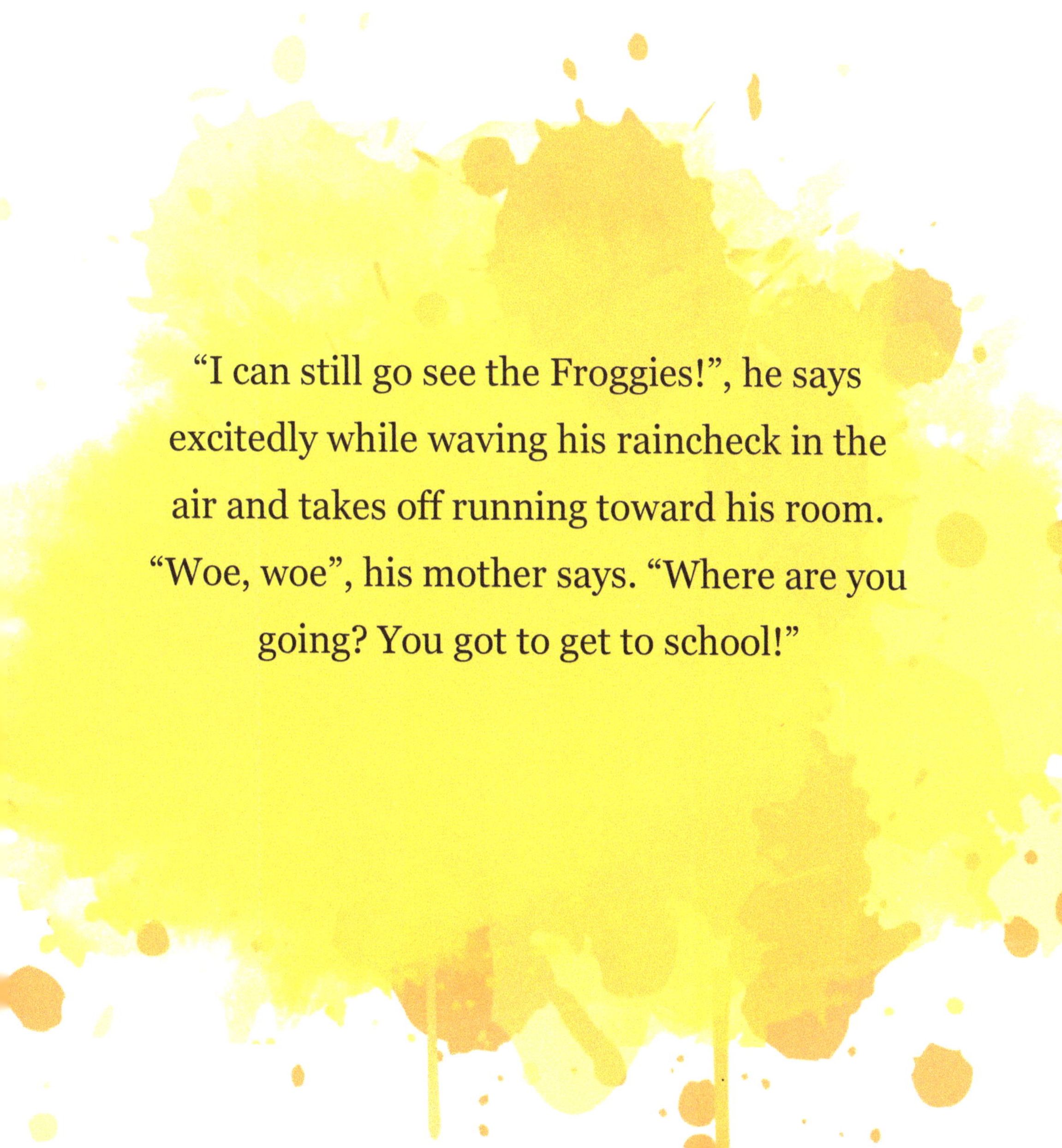

"I can still go see the Froggies!", he says excitedly while waving his raincheck in the air and takes off running toward his room. "Woe, woe", his mother says. "Where are you going? You got to get to school!"

"I know mom I got to run and see if God is available to tell him thank you before I head to school, Mom he may be booked up this afternoon!"

She stands in amazement and says, "Thank you God!"

As Henry Lee gets to the top of the steps, he stops and says, "Mom I will be right back, ok? I want to make sure he remembers Pete's raincheck as well."

With the biggest smile on her face, she simply responds, "No problem, dear take your time, take your time."

God
is a
forgiving
God

Rain Check FOR THIS
GOOD FOR
FORGIVEN
Date
REDEEMABLE BY Henry Lee
SIGNED God

Rain Check FOR THIS
GOOD FOR
FORGIVEN
Date
REDEEMABLE BY Anyone
SIGNED God

www.ingramcontent.com/pod-product-compliance
Lightning Source LLC
Chambersburg PA
CBHW042106160726
48295CB00017B/998